D1596461

melville house classics

THE ART OF THE NOVELLA

THE NICE OLD MAN AND THE PRETTY GIRL

THE NICE OLD MAN AND THE PRETTY GIRL

ITALO SVEVO

MELVILLE HOUSE PUBLISHING
BROOKLYN, NEW YORK

THE NICE OLD MAN AND THE PRETTY GIRL

TRANSLATED FROM ITALIAN BY L. COLLISON-MORLEY

ORIGINALLY PUBLISHED IN MILAN BY GIUSEPPE MORREALE, MILAN, 1929.

ORIGINALLY PUBLISHED IN ENGLISH BY
LEONARD AND VIRGINIA WOOLF AT THE HOGARTH PRESS,
LONDON, 1930.

MELVILLE HOUSE PUBLISHING

145 PLYMOUTH STREET

BROOKLYN, NY 11201

WWW.MHPBOOKS.COM

ISBN: 978-1-933633-89-3

FIRST MELVILLE HOUSE PRINTING: JULY 2010

BOOK DESIGN: KELLY BLAIR, BASED ON A SERIES DESIGN
BY DAVID KONOPKA

LIBRARY OF CONGRESS CATALOGING-IN-PUBLICATION DATA

SVEVO, ITALO, 1861–1928.
  [NOVELLA DEL BUON VECCHIO E DELLA BELLA FANCIULLA.
ENGLISH]
THE NICE OLD MAN AND THE PRETTY GIRL / ITALO SVEVO ;
[TRANSLATED FROM ITALIAN BY L. COLLISON-MORLEY]
    P. CM.
  ISBN 978-1-933633-89-3
  I. COLLISON-MORLEY, LACY, 1875– II. TITLE.
  PQ4841.C482N613 2010
  853'.8—DC22
                          2010011967

THE NICE OLD MAN AND THE PRETTY GIRL

I THERE was a prelude to the adventure of the nice old man, but it developed almost without his being aware of it. During a short break in his work he had been obliged to see in his office an old woman who introduced him to a girl in whom she tried to interest him, her own daughter. They had been granted an interview because they brought a letter from a friend of his. Called off thus suddenly from his work, the old man could not get it altogether out of his mind. He looked in bewilderment at the note, trying to take it in and put an end to the interruption as soon as possible.

The elder woman did not cease talking for a moment, but he caught or understood only a few short sentences: "The young woman was strong and intelligent, she could read and write, but she read better than she wrote." Then a sentence struck him, because it was so odd: "My daughter will take any work for the whole day, provided she has the short time off she needs for her daily bath." Finally the old woman made the remark which brought the scene to a swift close: "They are taking women as drivers and conductors on the trams now."

Quickly making up his mind, the old man wrote an introduction to the Manager of the Tramway Company and dismissed the two women. Left alone with his work, he interrupted it for a moment to think: "What on earth did that old woman mean by telling me that her daughter bathes every day?" He shook his head, smiling with an air of superiority. This shows that old men are really old when they have to do anything.

II A tram was running down the long Viale di Sant'Andrea. The driver, a pretty girl of twenty, kept her brown eyes fixed on the broad, dusty road, bathed in sun. She enjoyed driving the car at full speed, so that the wheels creaked when she changed gear and the body of the crowded tram jolted. The avenue was empty, but as she sped along the girl never ceased pressing her small nervous foot on the lever that rang the bell. This she did not as a precaution, but because she was young enough to be able to turn her work into a game, and she enjoyed going a good pace and making a noise with this amusing toy. All children like shouting when they run. She was dressed in old coloured clothes, which made her great beauty look as if disguised. A faded red jacket left free her neck, which was massive in comparison with her small, rather pinched face; free, too, the clean-cut hollow that runs from the shoulder to the delicate curve of the breasts. The blue skirt was too short, perhaps because in the third year of the war there was a scarcity of material. The tiny foot looked naked in a small cloth shoe and the blue cap crushed her black curls, which were cut short. Judged only by her head she might have been a boy, if the pose of that alone had not betrayed coquettishness and vanity.

On the footboard round the fair driver there were so many people that it was hardly possible to work the brakes. Among them was our old man. He had to bend backwards at some of the more violent jerks of the tram to prevent being shot on to the driver. He was dressed with great care, but in a sober style suited to his age. His appearance was really well bred and pleasing to the eye. Well-nourished though he was, among all these pale and anaemic people, there was nothing to give offence in him, because he was neither too fat nor too prosperous looking. From the colour of his hair and his short moustache you would have said he was sixty or rather less. There was no sign about him of an attempt to look younger. Years may be a hindrance to love, and for many years he had ceased to give it a thought, but they favour business, and he carried his years with pride, and, so to speak, youthfully.

On the other hand he had the caution of his years, and he was not happy in that gigantic car driven at such a pace. The first word he spoke to the girl was one of warning: "Signorina!"

At such polite language the girl turned her beautiful eyes towards him doubtfully, not being sure that he was addressing her. Her bright look gave the nice old man so much pleasure that his fears almost vanished. He changed the warning that would have had a touch of bitterness into a joke: "It makes no difference to me whether I am a minute or two sooner or later at the Tergesteo." The people round him might believe that he was smiling at his own joke, but as a matter of fact his smile had been directed towards her eye, which had struck him as full of delicious impertinence and at the same time innocent. Beautiful women always strike us at first as intelligent. A beautiful complexion or a beautiful line are, in fact, the expression of the highest intelligence.

She did not catch the words, but she was completely reassured by the smile that allowed no doubt as to the kindly feelings of the old man. She understood that he was uncomfortable standing and made room for him to lean upon the rail close by her. She kept on at breakneck speed to the Campo Marzo.

Then the girl, looking at the nice old man as if asking him to agree with her, sighed: "Here's where the real trouble begins." And the tram began to jolt slowly and heavily over the rails.

When a really young man falls in love, his love often sets up in his brain reactions that end by having nothing to do with his desire. How many young men who might enjoy peace and bliss in a hospitable bed, insist on abandoning at least their homes, in the belief that, in order to sleep with a woman, you must first conquer, create or destroy! Old men, on the other hand, who are said to be better protected against the passions, give themselves up to them in full knowledge and enter the bed of sin with no other precaution than a due regard for catching chills.

Not that love is simple, even for old men. For them its motives are complicated. They know that they must make excuses. Our old man said to himself: "This is my first real adventure since the death of my wife." In the language of the old an adventure is real when it involves the heart. It may be said that an old man is rarely young enough to be able to have an adventure that is not real, because this is an extension that serves to mask a weakness. Similarly, when weak men give a punch, they use not only the hand, the arm and the shoulder, but also the chest and the other shoulder. The blow is feeble owing to the excessive extension of the effort, while the adventure loses in distinctness and becomes more risky.

Then the old man thought that it was the child-like eye of the girl that had conquered him. Old men, when they fall in love, always pass through a stage of paternity and each embrace is an act of incest, carrying with it the bitter savour of incest.

And the third important idea the old man had when he felt himself deliciously guilty and deliciously young, was: "My youth is returning." So great is the selfishness of an old man that his thoughts do not remain fixed on the object of his love for a single moment without immediately turning back to contemplate himself. When he wants a woman, he is like king David, expecting to have his youth renewed by young girls.

The old man of classical comedy who is convinced that he can rival youth must be very rare today, if indeed he still exists. My old man continued to soliloquise and said to himself: "Here is a girl I shall buy, if she is for sale."

"Tergesteo—Are you not getting off?" asked the girl before starting the tram. The nice old man, rather confused, looked at his watch. "I shall go on a little further," he said.

There was no longer a crowd, and he had no further excuse for remaining so near the girl. He stood up and leant back in a corner whence he could see her comfortably. She must have been aware that she was being looked at, because, when she was not busy driving, she examined him curiously.

He asked her how long she had been at this tiring job. "A month." It was not so very tiring, she said, just as she was forced to lean the whole of her small body against a lever to apply the brake, but sometimes very dull. Worst of all, the pay was not enough. Her father still worked, but with food at such a price, it was hard to make ends meet. And, still intent upon her work, she addressed him by his surname: "If you liked, it would be easy for you to find me something better." She glanced quickly at him to judge from his expression the effect of her request.

The sudden use of his own name gave the nice old man rather a shock. The name of an old man is always a little ancient, and therefore imposes obligations on its bearer. He concealed all traces of strain that might betray his desire in his face. He was not surprised that the girl should know his name, because nearly all the richest families had left town, and the few well-to-do ones remaining were the more conspicuous. He looked away and said with great seriousness: "It is rather difficult now, but I will think it over. What can you do?" She could read and write and do accounts. The only languages she knew were Triestine and Friulian.

An old woman on the footboard began to laugh noisily: "Triestine and Friulian her only languages! Ah, that's good!" The girl laughed too, and the old man, still rigid from his efforts to conceal the excitement within him, laughed unnaturally. The peasant woman, pleased to talk with a gentleman of his position, kept up a continual chatter, and the old man encouraged her the better to appear indifferent. At last she left them alone. At once the old man exclaimed: "When are you off duty?"

"At nine in the evening."

"Well," said the nice old man, "Come this evening. I am engaged tomorrow." And he told her his address, which she repeated several times in order not to forget it.

Old men are in a hurry, because the law of nature as to the limits of age is threatening them. This rendezvous, asked for in the guise of a protecting philanthropist and accepted with gratitude, sent the old man into the seventh heaven of delight. How circumstances were playing into his hands!

But old men like to see clearly in business matters, and he could not yet bring himself to leave the footboard. Still doubting his luck, he asked himself anxiously: "Is this enough? Is there not something more to be done? Supposing she really believes that she has been asked to come for an introduction to get her another job?" He did not want to remain in a state of unnecessary excitement till the evening and would have liked to be more sure of his ground. But how utter the needful words without compromising his own family name, even with the girl, supposing that she really did not mean to take anything from him except a job? At bottom the position would have been the same had he been younger. But he was old. After a little experience, or even before they have had any, young men can get all they want, whereas the old man is a lover out of gear. The love-making machine within him is at least one little wheel short.

However, the old man was not inventing, but remembering. He remembered how at twenty, that is to say, forty years ago, before his marriage, he had whispered to a woman (much older than the tram-girl before him) who, on some flimsy pretext and in the presence of others, had already promised to come, in a low, but agitated voice a repetition of the invitation: "Will you come?' The words would have sufficed. But here the street, which envies the love of the young and laughs at that of the old, was watching him, and there must therefore be no trace of emotion in his voice.

As he was leaving the tram he said to the girl: "Then I shall expect you this evening at nine." Afterwards, as he remembered, he became aware that his voice, whether on account of the street or of his passion, had shaken. But he did not notice it at once, and when the girl answered: "Of course, I shan't forget to turn up," as she raised her eyes for a moment from the tram-lines and turned them towards him, it seemed to him that her promise had been made to the philanthropist. But, as he thought it over, all was as clear as forty years ago. The flash of her eye revealed the imp in her, as his own voice had revealed his anxiety. Without a doubt they understood each other. Mother Nature was graciously allowing him to love once again and for the last time.

III   The old man went off towards the Tergesteo with a more elastic step. He felt very fit, did the nice old man. Perhaps he had been without all that for too long. He had had so much to do that he had forgotten something which his system, still young, really needed. Feeling so fit, he could no longer have any doubt on the subject.

He was late when he reached the Tergesteo, so he had to hurry to the telephone to make up for lost time. For half an hour business absorbed his undivided attention. This calm was another source of satisfaction to him. He remembered how, when a young man, waiting had been such a torture and a delight to him that afterwards the pleasure awaited had paled by comparison. His calm seemed to him a proof of strength, and here he was certainly wrong.

When he had done his business he went towards the hotel where he always ate, like many other men of means who thus husbanded the supplies they had hoarded. He continued his self-examination as he walked. The desire within him was virile in its calmness, but complete. He had no scruples and he did not even remember how, when a young man, as became a person of refinement, every adventure of the kind had stirred within his breast the whole question of good and evil. He saw only one side of the problem, and it seemed to him that what he proposed taking was but his due, if only as a compensation for the long time during which he had been deprived of pleasure so great. As a rule most old men certainly believe that they have many rights and only rights. Knowing that they are beyond the reach of any education, they think they may live in accordance with the needs of their system. The nice old man sat down at the table with a desire for assimilating food that suggested real youth. "Lucky," he thought. "The glorious cure begins."

Yet, late in the afternoon, when, after leaving the office, the old man, in order to escape the dreary wait at home, went for a long walk by the sea and the jetty, there was a slight moral stirring in his breast which did not subside without leaving a trace in his heart. Not that this had the very least influence on the course of events, for, like other men, whether old or young, he did as he pleased, though he knew better.

The summer sunset was bright and pale. The sea, swollen, weary and motionless, looked colourless against the sky, still bright. The outlines of the mountains, dropping towards the Friulian plain, stood out clearly. There were even glimpses of the Hermada, and the air could be felt quivering with the ceaseless fire of the guns.

Every sign of the war that struck the old man reminded him, with a pang, that, thanks to it, he was making so much money. The war brought him wealth and humiliation. That day he thought: "And I am trying to seduce a girl of the people that is suffering and bleeding up there!" He had long grown accustomed to the remorse caused by his business success and he continued to make money, in spite of his remorse. His part of seducer was a new one and therefore the moral resistance was fresher and more intense. New crimes cannot be reconciled so easily with one's own highest moral convictions, and it takes time to make the two lie down together in amity, but there is no need for despair. Meanwhile there, on the jetty, within sight of the Hermada in flames, the nice old man gave up the idea. He would find his girl some healthy job and would be nothing but the philanthropist to her.

The hour of the meeting had nearly come. The moral struggle had made the task of waiting for her even less difficult. The idea of the philanthropist went home with the nice old man, though it left him the step of a conqueror which he had put on that morning as he left the footboard of the tram.

Even at home he did not abandon his purpose, but his actions belied it. To offer the girl a little supper was hardly the work of a philanthropist. He opened tins of nice food and prepared a choice little cold supper. On the table, between two glasses, he put a bottle of champagne. The time, however, was not very long.

Then the girl came. She was much better dressed than in the morning, but that did not alter matters, because she could not have made herself more desirable. In the presence of the sweets and the champagne the old man assumed a paternal aspect, to which the girl paid no attention, because she kept her innocent eyes fixed on the good supper. He told her he meant to have her taught a little German, which was necessary for the work, and then she made a remark that was decisive. She declared that she was ready to work the whole day on condition that she was allowed half an hour off for her bath.

The old man began to laugh: "Then we have known each other a long time. Are not you the girl who came to me with your mother? . . . How is the dear lady?"

The remark was really decisive, first of all because he learnt from it that they had known each other some time. Duration gives an adventure a more serious aspect. Then also the guarantee of the daily bath is, especially for an old man, of obvious importance. Even now he could hardly have understood, had he thought of it, why the girl's mother had mentioned the bath. The pose of the philanthropist vanished. He looked into her eyes laughing, as if meaning to laugh at his own moral struggles, seized her by the hand and drew her to him.

Then the old man would have liked to put on again at once his air of philanthropist. What was the use now of keeping up the odious appearance of seducer? He had the good taste to talk no more about jobs. Instead, he quickly gave her money. Then, after a slight hesitation, he gave her another separate sum, which he meant for that dear lady, her mother. To appear philanthropical, you must give also to the undeserving. Besides, old men always dole out their money in installments, whereas young men empty their pockets with a single gesture, only to repent later.

Thus the girl had the hard task of having to accept the money twice over and to pretend twice over that she did not want it. The first time is easy and it happens to them all. But the second time? She could not think of a different expression, as the occasion demanded, and repeated mechanically the words and the gestures she had used the first time. The third time too, she would have said: "Money? I don't want any," and would have taken it, saying: "I love you." After the second time she was a little troubled, and the old man attributed her trouble to her disinterestedness. But it may well be that she wondered whether the amount given her had been small and divided into two parts to make it seem larger.

This simple adventure became more complex in the excited brain of the nice old man. It is fate. Somehow or other, even when an old man pays, knowing that favours will no longer be given him, he always ends by falsifying his love adventures and soon earns the laugh of Beaumarchais and the music of Rossini. My nice old man—so intelligent—did not laugh at the words, simple as they were, of the young girl. The adventure must turn out to be "real" and he willingly lent his hand to the deceit. The girl was so charming that no word of hers could ring false. Now such falsifying had some importance, but only in the mind of the old man. Outwardly its only effect was to make the duration of that first interview, and also of those that followed, a little longer. If the old man had been able to do as he liked, he would have sent the girl away soon, because the immorality of old men is of short duration. But with a woman who loves, you cannot adopt such cavalier methods. He was not vain. He thought: "The girl loves the luxury of my office, of my house, of my person. Perhaps also she likes the gentleness of my voice and the refinement of my manners. She loves this room of mine where there is so much good food. She loves so many things of mine that she may love even me a little." The proffer of love is a very high compliment and pleases even when we don't know what to do with it. At worst it is at least the equivalent of the knightly titles of persons who deal in oxen, and we know how jealous they are of them. She told him, but without any intention of being tragic, that he was her first lover. And he believed it. In fact the nice old man had to put restraint on himself to prevent himself from offering her money for the third time. So willingly did he yield to the pleasure she gave him that he felt hurt when she told him that she did not like young men, and preferred old ones. This hearing himself called old was a rude awakening and it was painful to have to bow acknowledgments for the flattering declaration. However, the interview, even when least amorous, was anything but a torture to the nice old man. All the energies of the girl were concentrated upon devouring the good supper offered her, so that he could rest at his ease.

But he was glad to see her go and to be left alone. He was used to the talk of serious persons and it was impossible for him to endure long the foolish talk of the pretty girl. I shall be told that there are artists and thinkers, people more serious than my old business man, who, when young, endure with pleasure the chatter of a pretty mouth. But clearly old men are in certain respects more serious than the most serious young men.

The nice old man went to bed still a little troubled. When he was in bed he said: "We must think no more about her. Perhaps I shall never see her again."

So doubtful was he of his own love that he had arranged with her that he would send her a note of invitation for their next meeting.

Before going to sleep he was tortured with thirst. He had drunk too much and eaten things too highly spiced. He called his housekeeper, who brought him a glass of water and a reproachful glance. She was no longer very young, and it had always been her ambition to end up as mistress of the house. Then she had thought that the restraint of the old man arose from class feeling and had accepted the fact because one is born in one class or another without any fault of one's own. Now she had been able to see the girl for a moment when she left. This taught her that class feeling did not prevent the old man from doing anything. That was as good as a genuine slap in the face for her. Obviously the qualities that make a person more or less desirable do not depend on their merits or demerits. But she held that she possessed those qualities, and therefore it was the old man's fault if he did not recognise them.

IV   The note with which the old man invited the girl to another meeting was written a few days later, much sooner than he had imagined when he went to bed that night. He wrote to her with a smile on his face, satisfied with himself. He flattered himself that the second meeting would be even more fruitful in pleasure. Instead it was exactly like the first. When he dismissed the girl he was as cautious as before and arranged once more that she should come to him next when he sent for her. He invited her to the third meeting even more quickly, but the parting was the same. He never brought himself to arrange the next meeting at once. For the old man was always happy, both when he sent for the girl and when he dismissed her, that is, when he meant to return to the path of virtue. If, when he dismissed the girl, he had arranged the next meeting at once, this return to virtue would have been less genuine. In this way there was no idea of compromise, and his life remained orderly and virtuous with the exception of a very brief interval.

There would be little more for us to say about the interviews, if, after a time, the old man had not been seized with an insane jealousy—insane not for its violence, but for its strangeness. This is how it was. It did not appear when he wrote to the girl, because that was the moment when he was taking her away from the others; nor when he said good-bye to her, because that was the moment when he gave her over, willing and whole, to the others. In his case jealousy was inseparable from love, in space and time. Love was revived by it, and the adventure became more "real" than ever. A bliss and a pain indescribable. At a certain moment he became obsessed with the idea that the girl certainly had other lovers, all as young as he was old. He grieved over it for his own sake (oh, so much!), but also for hers, since she could thus throw away all hope of a decent life. It would be disastrous if she trusted others as she had trusted him. His own sin played its part in his jealousy. That is why, in order to make up for his own bad example, the old man habitually preached morality at the very moment when he was making love. He explained to her all the dangers of promiscuous love.

The girl protested that she had but one love, for himself. "Well," cried the old man, ennobled at one and the same time by love and morality, "if, in your desire to return to virtue, you had to decide not to see me again, I should be delighted." Here the girl made no answer, and for good reasons. For her the adventure was so clear that it was impossible for her to lie, as he did. She must not break off that relationship for the moment. It was also easy to keep silence when he was covering her with kisses. But when he gave vent to feelings more sincere and talked of other lovers, accusing her of having them, she found words again: How could he believe it? In the first place, she only went through the streets of the town on her tram, and besides, her mother kept an eye on her, and lastly, nobody wanted her, poor thing! And down fell a couple of tears. It was bad reasoning to use so many arguments, but in the meantime love and jealousy disappeared from the old man and she could go back to her supper.

This will show how old men regularly function. With young men each single hour is filled irregularly with the most diverse feelings, whereas with old men every feeling has its hour complete. The young girl fell in with the old man's ways. When he wanted her, she came; she went off when he had done with her. If they differed, they ended by making love and eating afterwards in the best of humours.

Perhaps the old man ate and drank too much. He was anxious to show off his strength.

I do not wish to imply that that is why the old man fell ill. Obviously an excessive number of years is more dangerous than an excess of wine, or of food or even of love. It may be that one of these excesses aggravated another, but it is not for me to assert even as much as that.

V He had gone quietly to bed, as he did every evening, and especially on those evenings when the girl left him, after eating everything that had been put before her.

He soon fell asleep. He afterwards remembered that he had dreamed, but so confusedly that he did not recollect anything about it. A number of people were round him, shouting, arguing with him and with each other. Then they had all gone away, and, utterly exhausted, he had thrown himself upon a sofa to rest. Then, on a little table exactly on a level with the sofa, he saw a large rat looking at him with its small bright eyes. There was laughter, or rather mockery, in those eyes. Then the rat vanished, but to his horror he realized that it had forced its way into his left arm, and, digging furiously, was making for his chest, causing him excruciating pain.

He woke up gasping, covered with perspiration. It had been a dream, but something real remained behind, the excruciating pain. The image of the object causing the pain changed immediately. It was no longer a rat, but a sword fixed in the upper part of the arm, the point of which reached his chest; curved, not cutting, but jagged and poisonous, because it caused pain wherever it touched. It prevented him from breathing or making any movement. It would have been possible to break the sword by wrenching it, if he had moved. He shouted and he knew it, because the effort of making himself heard hurt his throat, but he was not sure that he heard the sound he uttered. There was a great deal of noise in that empty room. Empty? In that room was death. A profound darkness drew towards him from the ceiling, a cloud which, when it reached him, would crush out of him the little breath that was still left, and would cut him off for ever from all light, driving him among things base and filthy. The darkness drew slowly nearer. When would it reach him? Without a doubt it might expand at any moment, wrap itself round him and strangle him in a second. Was this what death, which had been familiar to him from childhood, was like? So insidious and bringing with it so much pain? He felt the tears flowing from his eyes. He wept from fear and not in the hope of awakening pity, because he knew that there was no pity. And the terror was so great that he seemed to himself to be without fault or sin. He was being strangled like this, he so good and gentle and merciful.

How long did the terror last? He could not have said, and he might have imagined that it lasted a whole night, if the night had not been so long. It seemed to him that first the threatening darkness left him and then the pain. Death had vanished, and the next day he would welcome the sun again. Then the pain shifted, and there was instant relief. It was driven higher up towards the throat, where it disappeared. He covered himself up with the blankets. His teeth chattered with cold, and a convulsive shivering prevented him from resting. But the return to life was complete. He did not call out again, and he was glad that his cry had not been heard. His housekeeper, nasty creature, would have thought that his illness was due to the visit of the girl on the previous evening. This is how he came to remember her, and suddenly he thought: "No more love-making for me!"

VI   The doctor, who was called in in the morning, examined him, and thought the matter over, but did not at first attach much importance to the attack. The old man described the adventure of the previous evening, including the food and the champagne, and the doctor thought that the trouble was due to these excesses. He said he was sure the trouble would not return, provided the old man lived quietly, taking regularly every two hours a certain powder, and refrained from seeing the object of his passion or even from thinking of her.

The doctor, who was a contemporary and an old friend, treated him without any ceremony: "My dear fellow, you must not go to your lover until I allow you."

The old man, however, who attached more importance to his health than the doctor, thought: "Even if you gave me permission, I would not go to her. I was so much better before I knew her."

As soon as he was alone, he began to think of the girl, with the idea of freeing himself from her altogether. But he remembered that the girl loved him, and he therefore thought her capable of coming to see him after a time, even without being invited. The strength of love is well known. Then what sort of a figure would he cut, he who had determined not to see her even with the doctor's permission? He wrote to her that he should have to leave town unexpectedly for a long time. He would let her know when he returned. He enclosed a sum of money which was meant to settle accounts with his own conscience. The letter also ended with a kiss, written after a moment's hesitation. No. The kiss had not set his pulse beating.

The next day he felt reassured by a quiet, though almost sleepless night. The terrible pain had not returned, whereas, in spite of the doctor's assurances, he had dreaded being attacked by it every night in the dark. Next time he went to bed more calmly and recovered confidence, but not sleep. The rumbling of the guns reached him and the nice old man asked: "Why have they not managed to discover a way of killing each other without making so much noise about it?" It was not very long since the day when the sound of the fighting had awakened generous impulses in him. But illness had taken from him the remnants of a feeling for his fellows which old age had failed to destroy in him.

During the next few days the doctor added some drops in the intervals between the powders. Then, to insure his sleeping at night, he came in the evening to give him injections. There was also special medicine for the appetite which he had to take at stated hours. There was plenty to do in the old man's day. And the housekeeper, unnoticed in happier days, became very important. The old man, who could be grateful, might perhaps have grown fond of her, for sometimes she had even to get up in the night to give him his medicines. But she had a bad fault. She did not forgive him his transgressions and made frequent references to them. The first time she had to give him a small dose of champagne by way of medicine, she accompanied it with the remark: "It is some of that which was bought for a very different purpose."

For a time the old man protested, trying to make her think that between him and the girl there had been nothing more than an affection of the utmost purity. Then, seeing that nothing could shake her conviction, he began to believe that she had long known it and had spied upon him. How could he tell when? He puzzled his brains for a long while to find out. He blushed especially for what the woman knew, because the rest did not exist, but with that damned woman everything ended by existing, given those very vague allusions of hers, with the help of which it was possible to remember the whole adventure. The result was that he could no longer endure the woman and allowed her near him only when he needed her. It is true that he needed her also to gossip with, so that even this hatred, which might have been really vital, was ineffectual. It confined itself to his whispering to the doctor: "She is as ugly as sin."

In the course of his struggle with this woman he remembered the girl, but without regretting her. All he regretted was his health, or rather what he regarded as his own youth. Youth had fled with the girl's last visit, and regret for this persisted in his regret for her. Now, in all seriousness, he would find a job for the girl . . . if he recovered his health. Then he would return to his important and profitable work and not to sin. It was sin that injured health.

Summer passed. He was allowed to go for a drive on one of the last calm days. The doctor went with him. The result was far from unfavourable, for he enjoyed the change and his condition was no worse, but it was impossible to repeat the experiment in the bad weather that followed.

Thus his empty life went on. There was no change, except in the medicines. Each medicine was good for a time. Then the doses had to be increased to produce the same effect till it had to be replaced by another drug. After a month or two, it is true, they began all over again.

However, a certain equilibrium was established in his system. If he was going to his death, the progress was imperceptible. It was no longer a question of the pain, heroic in its violence, on the night when death had uplifted its arm to give him the decisive blow. Far from it. Perhaps, as he was then, he was no longer worth striking. He thought he was getting better every day. He even believed that his appetite had returned. He took time to swallow his tasteless broths and really thought he was eating. There were still some tins of stimulating food in the house. The old man took one in his trembling hands: he read the name of the famous maker and put it down again. He meant to keep it for the day when he should be even better. For that day were also kept some bottles of champagne. It had been found that the wine was useless for his malady.

The most important part of the day was that which he spent by a window during the warmest hours. That window was a chink through which he looked out on life as it went on its way in the streets, even now that he had been exiled from it. If the woman of sin, as he called her, was at hand, he criticized to her the luxury that still appeared in the poor streets of Trieste or pitied in rather emphatic tones the poverty that went by in a stream. Opposite his house was a baker's and there was often a queue of people drawn up at his door, waiting for their crust of bread. The old man expressed pity for these people waiting so anxiously for a badly cooked loaf that filled him with disgust, but here his pity was pure hypocrisy. He envied those who moved freely about the streets. It was childish of him. On the whole he was comfortable in the shelter of his well-warmed room, but he would have liked to look even beyond that road. The passers-by who awakened his curiosity, because they were dressed either too well or too badly, turned round the corner and were lost to him.

One night when he could not sleep he began to walk about the room and, in his desire to move and to find some distraction, he went to the window. The queue by the baker's door was already there, so long that even at night it stained the pavement with black. Even then he did not really pity these people who were sleepy and could not go and sleep. He had a bed and could not sleep. Those waiting in the queue were certainly better off.

These were the days of Caporetto. His doctor gave him the first news of the disaster. He had come to weep in the company of his old friend, whom he (poor doctor!) believed to be capable of feeling as he did. Instead the old man could see nothing but good in what had happened: the war was moving away from Trieste and therefore from him. The doctor wailed: "We shan't see even their aeroplanes any longer." The old man muttered: "True, probably we shan't see them any more." In his heart he rejoiced at the prospect of quiet nights, but he tried to copy the pain he saw in the doctor's face in his own expression.

In the afternoon, when he felt up to it, he interviewed his confidential manager, an old clerk who enjoyed his complete confidence. In business the old man was still sufficiently energetic and clear-headed, and the clerk came to the conclusion that the old man's illness was not very serious and that he would come back to work sooner or later. But his energy in business was of the same kind as that which he displayed in looking after his health. The slightest indisposition was sufficient to make him put off business to the next day. And for the sake of his health he managed to forget business the moment his clerk was gone. He sat down by the stove into which he liked to throw bits of coal and watch them burn. Then he shut his dazzled eyes and opened them to go on with the same game. This is how he passed the evenings of days which had been quite as empty.

But his life was not to end in this way. Some organisms are fated to leave nothing behind them for death, which merely succeeds in seizing an empty shell. All that he could burn, he burnt, and his last flame was the finest.

VII   The old man was at his window, looking out on to the road. It was a dull afternoon. The sky was covered with a greyish mist, and the pavement wet, though it had not rained for two days. The queue of hungry customers was forming in front of the baker's door.

As luck would have it, the girl went by at that very moment in front of the balcony he was occupying. She had no hat on, but the old man, who would not have known how to describe a single detail of her dress, thought her better dressed than in the days when he loved her. With her was a young man, fashionably dressed to the point of exaggeration. He wore gloves and carried a smart umbrella, which he raised two or three times with the arm with which he was gesticulating in accompaniment to his talk, which was clearly lively. The girl, too, was laughing and chatting.

The old man looked and sighed. It was no longer the life of others that was passing along the street, it was his own. And the old man's first instinct was one of jealousy. There was no question of love, only the most abject jealousy: "She is laughing and enjoying herself while I am ill." They had done wrong together, and the resulting illness had come upon him; upon her, nothing. What was to be done? She was walking with her light step and would soon be at the corner, where she would disappear. That was why the old man sighed. There was not even time to disentangle his own thoughts, and he felt such a longing to speak to her and give her a moral lecture.

When the girl and her companion disappeared the old man tried to check his excitement, as it might be bad for him, and said: "All the better. She is alive and enjoying herself." There were two lies in those few words, which implied first of all that the old man had worried what had happened to the girl during his illness, then that it gave him satisfaction to see her running about the streets in that way enjoying herself. Therefore he could not get her out of his mind. He remained by the window and looked in the direction where the girl had disappeared. If she had come back, he would have called to her from the window. It was not very cold, and he felt that he must see her. And a voice within him asked him suspiciously: "Why? Do you want to begin all over again?" The old man began to laugh: "Desire? Not a thought of it!" Yet he continued looking in the same direction in an attitude of the most intense longing. "I should be quite happy," he thought, convinced this time that he was speaking the truth, "if I knew that the young man loves her and means to marry her."

No one, not even himself, could have unravelled completely the old man's mind, passionately dissatisfied as he was with the girl and with himself. He saw clearly that the girl's behaviour involved responsibility of his own. This he tried to diminish by remembering that he had preached morality to her, and the rest he tried to forget. To recover his peace of mind he must impress upon her more clearly (that is, upon her, for he asked nothing for himself) the moral precepts she might have forgotten. And there was the further danger that she had forgotten his words and not his actions.

He hurried to the desk to write to her, bidding her come and see him. Why not? He would receive her calmly, like his employees from the office, and urge her to think more seriously about her future.

With the pen in his hand, he found himself in difficulties. He wanted to make it clear to her at once that this letter was not from a lover, but from a respectable old man who was inviting her to come and see him for her own good. He took a calling card and wrote a couple of words of invitation under his own name. He left the card on his desk and went back to the window. It would be better if she came down the street again. There was the risk that she would not accept this invitation, which would seem strange to her. But it was important that she should come, important for him.

He went back to the desk and wrote her again the same note he had sent her so often. He blushed scarlet, because his fault was thus actually called up again in tangible form. But he need not stand on ceremony with that girl. It was enough to induce her to come in order to put her out of his life; and to wipe out from his destiny a presence so inconvenient, he considered that all that was necessary was to tell her distinctly (more distinctly than he had been able to do in the past): "For my part, I ask you to behave yourself with me and with all other men." Then it would be easy to think no more about her.

He tried to find peace in making his own resolution decisive. He found a way to send the note without letting it pass through the hands of his nurse. The appointment was for the morrow, in the late hours of the afternoon. The early hours were taken up with his cures.

He returned to the window. In his desire to clear his conscience of all stain he went over in his mind the story of his relations with the girl. It would be strange to attach any importance to it. She had been too easy a conquest. A very commonplace adventure.

Not in his own life, however, and important also for the youth and beauty of the girl. "Undoubtedly the others are worse than I am, and to-day I am superior to them all." He felt that he could be proud of not feeling any desire and even more proud of sending for the girl to do her good.

He would give her money. How much? Two, three, five hundred kronen. He must give her the money if only to acquire the right to educate her. Then he would put her on her guard against promiscuous loves. He had already preached to her against such loves in the past, but now he must make her forget that he had then tried to include his love among the permissible.

A scene occurred in the street that riveted his whole attention. He had seen the actors a long way off, because they came from the quarter he was watching. A boy of about eight or ten, barefooted, was coming down the street, dragging after him by the hand a man who was evidently drunk. The child seemed to be aware of his responsibility. He was walking with small, but resolute steps. Every now and then he looked back at the full-grown man behind him, who appeared to realize that he must follow him, then he looked in front of him to see where he was going. Clearly he knew that he had to take command and lead the way. In this way they came under the old man's window. There the child stepped off the pavement in order to get along better, but the man did not follow him at once. Thus it happened that their linked arms caught against a lamp-post. The child did not realise at once that he would have to go back to keep hold of the man. He was in a hurry, and probably he hurt the drunken man by pressing his arm against the lamp-post. The man was seized with a sudden fury. He broke loose from the boy and kicked him, knocking him down. Luckily he was too drunk to move quickly, because it was obvious that he was drawing back to strike again. The boy, on the ground, covered his face in childish fashion with his arm and cried, looking terror-stricken at the drunken man who was bending over him without being able to recover his balance.

The old man at the window was filled with terror. He opened the window, forgetting for the moment the danger to his own health, and began to call for help in his harsh voice. A number of people ran over at once from the queue at the baker's door, so many that very soon the old man could see neither the child nor the drunken man. He shut the window again, called for his nurse, and sank, gasping for breath, into an arm-chair. It was too much for him. His legs gave way under him.

During his long solitude he had nursed a great ambition and had thought himself beneficent and superior to everyone else, but now for the first time he was experiencing a sensation, really new and surprising, one of genuine, instinctive goodness. For a short while he remained good and generous without any thought of himself obscuring this feeling. It is quite true that he took no step to bring the poor child in need of help and comfort nearer to him. The idea never crossed his mind; but in his thoughts he dwelt affectionately and with deep emotion upon the childish figure that had been knocked down. He even discovered in his own memory a detail that helped to increase his pity: he had seen the boy crying, but he had not heard a single sound. Perhaps the little boy was ashamed of being punished in public, and the shame, which prevented him from attracting the attention of others, was stronger than his terror. Poor little thing, thus made even more helpless.

But very soon the old man returned to his regular occupation of looking after himself. Meanwhile his generous feelings had had such an expansive effect upon his heart that he immediately recognized the good result of his impulsive action. In order to keep it up he talked to the nurse about his great adventure. He said that he had saved the child. "If I had not shouted, that blackguard would have made an end of him." As a matter of fact, it is quite likely that his hoarse cry never reached the street.

In his thoughts he went back to the girl and set up in his mind a kind of association between the boy who was being ill-used and the young woman who, in the same street, was being dragged to her ruin by a smart young rake. His pity for the boy made him even blame himself for not having done more for him than open the window and shout.

He put this thought from him by thinking: "I have one misfortune to think of, and that is enough for me."

That night he had no sleep till the morning. He had no pain, and he lay thinking. He was well aware that his conscience was not at ease, but he could not see why. He decided to give the girl an even larger sum. He thought that, if he could make her declare herself grateful, it would be enough to set his own conscience at rest.

Towards morning he fell asleep and had a dream. He was walking in the sunlight, holding the pretty girl by the hand, exactly as the drunken man was holding the boy's hand. She also was walking a little in front of him and he was thus able to see her better. She was very pretty, dressed in bright-coloured old clothes, as on the first day he had seen her. As she walked, she beat her little foot on the ground, and at each step the warning bell rang, as on that day on the Viale di Sant'Andrea. The old man, who had till then been walking with his usual slow step, forced himself to catch the girl up. She had become for him the woman of his desire, all of her, with her old clothes, her step and even the silver note of the bell that must have been fastened to her little foot. Then suddenly he became tired and wanted to let go the girl's hand. But he did not succeed till he fell exhausted to the ground. The girl moved away from him like an automatic figure without even glancing at him, with the same step, which was musical with the ringing of the bell. Was she taking her sex to others? In the dream that was a matter of complete indifference to him. He woke up. He was bathed in perspiration, as on that night of the bad attack of angina. "Disgusting, disgusting!" he exclaimed, thoroughly frightened at his own dream. He tried to calm himself by remembering that a dream has nothing to do with the man who has it, but is sent him by mysterious powers. But the disgusting details were clearly his own. Undoubtedly he felt more remorse for his dream than for the recent reality in which he had played a part. While he was busy looking after his health, a duty which took up the whole morning, though he was unable to throw off the memory of the night's adventure, he was seized with an inspiration: between the boy knocked down and beaten and the girl of his dream mechanically offering her beauty there was an analogy. "And between me and the drunken man?" queried the old man. He tried to smile at the impossible comparison. Then he thought: "However, I can make reparation by helping her and teaching her better."

During the day he was assailed by further doubts. Supposing he had really behaved as he behaved in the dream? It may be that dreams are sent by others and that we are not in any way responsible for them, but he was old enough to know that even in real life, sometimes, in certain actions, we cannot recognise ourselves. For instance, he had begun his adventure after that historical walk on the jetty, when his intentions had been very different. Now, if his present intentions were worth no more than those, there was an end of peace, an end of health and certainly also an end of life.

Then the old man took a truly heroic decision. He determined to sacrifice his life rather than continue to live his present lonely existence in the midst of his chemist's shop. To-day, especially after his dream, he felt even more desirous to live and act. To-day, if he had again been a spectator of the cruel treatment of the little boy, he would not have been able to sink down and rest, as on the day before. He even thought that, when he had cleared up his position with the girl, he might find the young man also and do him some good. Only just now matters were too involved and he would have to wait for the visit of some influential friend whom he could employ to make the needful inquiries. The old man gave no thought to all the other boys in similar circumstances who were within easy reach of him, and he soon forgot the one he loved because he had seen him beaten.

He told the doctor something of his nocturnal adventure. His old friend, who managed every day to find some symptom of a speedy recovery, smiled:

"Why, you are getting well; you are even getting young again."

"Is that how health and youth begin?" asked the old man, perplexed. He had no used for such youth. He wanted peace, quiet, real health. Above all he wanted to rid himself of all self-reproach for his behaviour towards the girl. The doctor could not guess that his patient had then decided to cure himself in his own way, especially as the old man would not have known how to tell him. He himself did not know that he was running after a new cure.

In the afternoon the old man enjoyed a long, refreshing, dreamless sleep. He awoke smiling like a child from a sleep that was at last innocent, because untroubled by images.

Then he prepared supper for the girl, exactly as he had done the first time he had waited for her. Before beginning his work he had a momentary hesitation. But then he thought that sooner or later the girl would have to listen to his hard words and to less amusing sermons and that therefore it was right to give her the reward by which she apparently set so much store. So he carefully opened the tins he had kept by him so long. He smiled as he emptied the contents on to the plates that were ready on the usual little table. It was a question of gilding a pill which the girl might find bitter.

His nurse was alarmed at seeing all these preparations. Was it not her duty to warn the doctor? The old man reassured her with an air of superiority. His last sleep had been peaceful and he had forgotten the one before. Hence the nurse's suspicions could not even offend him. He told her that she might listen to the interview in the next room. For the first time he spoke openly of the past, confessing what she probably knew or had at least suspected. "Youthful transgressions must be forgotten. In any case they cannot be repeated." But the nurse was not satisfied. Though she wanted for nothing in that house, she did not like to see all this good food prepared for someone else. She answered venomously: "Then five months ago you were young?"

"Was it only five months ago?" asked the old man in amazement. To him it seemed a century since the girl's last visit. He made the necessary calculations and discovered that it was even less than five months since it all happened. He made no answer to the nurse, but he could not believe that he was old when he had been so young five months ago. However, he had no doubt of his own sincere wish to be moral and good.

VIII   The girl was, as always, punctual. The old man had felt none of the nervousness in waiting for her he had experienced in the past. This comforted him. If his dream had presaged sexual excitement, the reality—he was now convinced of it—was something entirely different. But the violent emotion he experienced at seeing once again the girl's dear face was a great surprise to him. Now he realized that it was out of the question for him to assume with her, as he had intended doing, the airs of the head of an office. He nearly fainted. How enchanting was that little face with the great eyes, every line of which he knew from having kissed it, and how musical was that voice he had heard while he was behaving in a way that now filled him with remorse. He could not find words to welcome her and for a long while he held the little gloved hand in his own. It was so good to love. Was a new, a last youth beginning for him? A new cure, more effective than all the others?

Then he looked at her. Her face seemed less fresh. Round her mouth, which five months ago he had compared to a flower scarcely budding, some of the lines had altered. Horizontally the mouth had lengthened a little and the lips seemed less full. Some bitterness? Perhaps some rancour against him? Because—only now did he remember it—he had promised love and protection and then suddenly he had repudiated all his promises to her. Hence the first words he uttered were to ask her forgiveness. He told her how, at the time when he had written her her that he must leave town, he had really been ill. He described the great attack of angina, which now lay so far behind him, as if it had been yesterday. In a way, therefore, he lied, but only so as to insure being immediately forgiven.

She, however, had no thought of a grievance against him. Far from it. She had immediately made as if she would kiss him right on the mouth. He offered her his cheek and just touched hers with his own lips. "What a pity," she said; "it would have been better if you had gone away instead of being ill."

In order to see her better, he made her sit down at the other end of the table. It must have been ordained by mother Nature that old men should see better at a distance, because there is no object in their having things within reach.

Suddenly he noticed with surprise that the curls which he had seen flying free in the air on the previous day were now covered with a smart hat, adorned with good feathers of sober hue. Why this transformation, as it might be called in Trieste, where a woman's hat shows exactly the class to which she belongs? She came to him in a hat, while she did not wear one when walking in the street? It was strange. And how different was her style of dress! She was no longer a daughter of the people; she belonged to the middle classes in her hat, her well-cut dress and its ample material, such as was then the fashion, when material was scarce. To the middle classes, too, if not to the best of them, belonged the transparent silk stockings, which were such a poor protection to the legs against the cold, and the little varnished shoes. It was not merely affection that made it impossible for the old man to adopt the rather stern air he had intended, but also, to some extent, respect. She was certainly the smartest person he had talked to for a long time. He, on the other hand, was dressed very slackly. He had not even got on his collar, because it made him short of breath. Instinctively he put his hand to his throat to see whether he had buttoned his shirt.

Where could all the money have come from to buy all this finery? Instead of thinking what he had to say, the old man lost himself in calculations. How much money had he sent her five months ago? Could the money he had given her have been enough to explain all this luxury?

She looked at him smiling, and seemed to be waiting. He had already decided not to assume for the moment the appearance of a mentor, especially as he seemed to be admonishing her sufficiently by setting an example of virtue. That is why he could not think of anything else to say than to ask "Are you still on the trams?"

At first she seemed not to understand: "On the trams?" Then she appeared to recollect: It was not work suited to a young girl. She had left it some time ago.

He invited her to eat. It was a way of gaining time, because he was wondering whether he ought not to have reproved her for giving up work. While she was preparing to eat, slowly taking off her gloves, he asked her: "And what are you doing now?"

"Now?" asked the girl, hesitating in her turn. Then she smiled: "Now I am looking for a job, and you must find me one."

"I shall be delighted," said the old man. "As soon as I am well, I will take you into my office. Have you learnt any German?" "Ah, German!" she said, laughing heartily. "We two began to love each other with German, and we might go on learning it together." This was a suggestion he pretended not to hear.

She began to eat, but in a most self-possessed way. Knife and fork worked with complete ease and the mouthfuls reached the dainty mouth in due measure, whereas at the early suppers to which he had invited her the little fingers had also had to assist in breaking up the food and conveying it to its destination. The old man felt that he ought to be gratified at finding her so much more refined.

He was still hesitating. If he went on laughing and smiling with her, what was going to happen? In order not to give offence he meant to speak only of his own fault: "If that day I had got into conversation with you only to give you advice for your own good. . . ."

The girl's simple common sense at this point raised an objection which was to weigh upon the old man even later: "But if you had not fallen in love with me, you would not have accosted me at all." And he realized at once that if he had not been kept on the foot-board of the tram by his desire, he would have got off at the Tergesteo without even noticing that the girl might need him.

She had not taken his words very seriously, because she said at once: "Was I pretty on the tram? Tell me now, you liked me very much?" She got up, went to him and stroked his cheek, which had been shaved that day. What could he do but return the caress by putting his hand under her chin?

He tried to take up the thread of his speech. "I was too old for you, and I ought to have known it."

"Old!" she exclaimed in protest. "I loved you because I liked that air of distinction of yours." He was forced to smile at the compliment, and he was really pleased. He knew that even in his old age he looked distinguished and he took pride in the fact.

"But if," she added, eating, "you want to adopt me as your daughter, there is plenty of time. Should not I make a lovely daughter?"

Unbounded assurance came out in every word she said, and it seemed to him that the girl of the people had been different. In her old clothes, at the very moment when she had seduced him, she had been so much more moral. While she was eating she managed to stretch herself on the arm-chair and display her legs with their smart stockings to the gaze of the old man. Adopt her? A girl who showed him legs about which he did not care twopence?

Anger made him more eloquent. "That day I accosted you with the idea of doing you good and leading you to a better life. Do you remember how I spoke to you about jobs and lessons? Do you remember? Then passion gained the mastery. But remember that, on the very first evening, I wanted to speak to you again about work, and I spoke about it on the second and always, every time I saw you. Then I also told you to be on your guard, and not let yourself be inveigled into other irregular amours. Do you remember?" He had thus admitted, and without the slightest effort, that his own love had also been irregular.

And he breathed again. Seeing that the girl remembered everything he wanted and nothing else, he breathed again. It seemed to him that he was cleared of all reproach, and he thought now that he would be able to devote himself to teaching the girl morality, without finding any impediment in the example he himself had set. With his nurse he had been more honest and had excused his earlier transgressions by his youth. With the girl, on the contrary, he was trying to wipe out those transgressions by means of the words with which he had accompanied them.

Apparently he had succeeded, and he was inexpressibly pleased in consequence. He thought he could look at the whole world objectively now that he was at last free of all the compromising circumstances to which all men are driven by their own weaknesses. If he had really been the objective observer he imagined, he might have seen that there was still something of the girl of the people in this girl, something simple and ingenuous, and delighted in it. She went on eating with a good appetite and said she remembered everything he wanted her to remember and nothing he did not want. She had not the slightest idea why he talked as he did, but she was not surprised at his words. She would not have been in the least surprised if he had then begun to kiss her and embrace her, as in the past. It might well be that, whereas in the past he had been in the habit of making love first and preaching afterwards, he had decided, after his bad illness, to begin with the sermon, and it was not her business to understand the reason for the change.

However, she declared that she had always followed his advice, and had never given herself up to irregular loves. She spoke calmly, continuing to eat and not paying the slightest attention to the face of her interlocutor to see whether he believed her.

He did not believe her, but he felt obliged to appear a little grateful, because she had been so forbearing with him. "Bravo," said he, "I am very pleased with you. You are doing me the greatest kindness in remaining honest, and you will see that I shall be very grateful." He imagined that he had done a great deal in that first interview. The rest might be held over till the next day, after he had had the necessary time for reflection. Yet he could not manage to change the subject, not merely because old men are rather like crocodiles, which cannot easily change their direction, but also because there was now only one link between him and the girl. There had in fact never been more than one between them, only now it was a different one. "And how about the young man you were with yesterday under my window?"

She did not remember at once that she had gone down that street. She recollected after an effort of memory, or rather of thought. She must have gone down that road when she came to the other one from her home. The young man was a cousin of hers back from the university. There was no need to take the boy seriously.

Again he did not believe her, but he thought that for the moment it would be better not to press the point. Before dismissing her, on the pretext that he was very tired, he gave her money, this time not in an envelope, but counted out carefully on the table. He looked at the girl, expecting to enjoy her thanks. He did not notice much. First of all it disgusted her to talk of money always, and the old man had to ask her more than once to help him count it, because she was looking the other way; then, after all, there was not much of it, for in those days it was only just enough to buy the shoes the girl was wearing.

She went off after giving him a good, long kiss, and certainly thought that the love was being held over till the second meeting.

IX   When the old man wanted to set his thoughts in order, he was in the habit of chatting with the person nearest to hand. This was therefore always his enemy and his one companion, his nurse. So he told her that he felt pleased that the girl had remembered even the moral lessons he had given her in the past, nor was he stopped by the evil glance of surprise his nurse shot him. He told her good-humouredly, as if he were thinking aloud, that he now meant to help the girl, and even mentioned the amount of money he had given her that day.

His nurse started. The mention of the girl always brought out the bad in her, but she began by expressing contempt for the money, which he had thought a considerable sum. As we shall see, she was not clever, but she was then pursuing a line of her own in an attempt to get her wages raised. As a matter of fact the old man had not yet realised that the value of money had fallen lower than ever. Then she added, "As for her"—the vague wave of the hand indicated the girl—"it is easy for her to remember the noble moral lessons you have given her; I've no doubt they did her a great deal of good."

This second remark was less important to the old man than the first. He was deeply concerned at having tainted himself with meanness when he had meant to behave so generously. If what his nurse said was true, he had made a great mistake, because he meant the money to represent his own ransom, which could not be paid with a small sum.

This was his first reason for dissatisfaction after being so confident of attaining peace. At bottom remorse is only the effect of a certain way of looking at one's self in a mirror. And he saw himself mean and small. He had always paid the girl too little. For some pleasures generous men saddle themselves with equivalent responsibilities. In order not to saddle himself with any he remembered that in the past he had never even made appointments with her beforehand, so that, when he had had enough of her, all he had to do was not to send for her. Other men pay women every day, since they must eat, even when nothing is wanted of them. He, on the other hand, had allowed her to work on the trams, in order to earn her daily bread; and yet he had paid her in a way which had seemed to him princely, because it had not occurred to him that he owed her more than the hire of a few hours. That his how he had managed this adventure which, in his desire to gloze over its shady aspects, he had insisted on calling "real".

And this seemed to him to be the real cause for remorse, not the fact that he, an old man, had had an affair with a young girl. Why should he have felt remorse if he had taken the girl to live with him and had given her the place of his hateful nurse? The old man smiled, a little bitterly it is true, but he smiled. The girl always at his side! The great attack of angina would have occurred much sooner. Not now, because he was sure that he could live in the closest contact with the girl without fearing any temptation. He was annoyed that she still put on her siren airs with him, and that was why he could not have endured her near him.

But in the past, since he had loved her, it was his duty to have kept her with him and then she would have been better educated. That is what young men did, whereas old men loved and ran away or drove away the loved object from them.

How absurd he must have been, when he forced her to help count over the large sum he was offering her. But that he could make good. He immediately told his clerk to let him have a really considerable sum of money for the next day.

In other ways, too, he might make reparation. Since he felt for her nothing but a paternal affection,

68

ITALO SVEVO

he might attempt to educate her. He felt up to it. Only he must prepare himself carefully before meeting her. Now he had no further desire to remind her of the silly words with which he used to accompany the manifestations of his own corruptness. He had been weak with her, because he was still always possessed by the mad desire to appear pure.

For some time longer he sat thinking in the armchair. It would have been so nice to explain his intentions to someone else before putting them into practice. Even in business he was in the habit of talking matters over with his solicitor so as to get a clear idea of what he intended to do. But in this matter, which he was managing alone, he could not ask anyone's advice. Certainly he could not speak of it to his nurse.

And that is how, late in life, my nice old man became an author. That evening he wrote only notes for the lecture he meant to give the girl. They were sufficiently short. He described his own faults without trying to attenuate them. He had meant to make use of her and slip out of all responsibility towards her. These were his two faults. It was so easy to write them. Would he have the pluck to repeat it all to the girl? Why not, when he was ready to pay? Pay in money and pay in himself, that is, to educate her and act as her guardian. That young rake would not find his game quite so easy. Thus, as he wrote, there swam into his ken one who also ought to have had his share in the pain and remorse of the old man.

These notes were first written in pencil, then copied carefully in ink. There was no risk for manuscripts in that room, because his nurse could not read. When he wrote them out in ink, he added a moral of more general application, rather dull and rhetorical. He believed himself that he had improved and completed his work, whereas he had spoilt it. But this was inevitable in a novice. In the past the old man had been a sceptic. Now that his illness had thrown his organism out of gear, he was aware of a proclivity towards protecting the weak, and at the same time an inclination for propaganda. He believed all of a sudden that he had a message to give, and not to the girl alone.

He read over his manuscript and, truth to tell, he was disillusioned. Not altogether, however, because he thought that his ideas were good, but that he had expressed them badly. This fault he would be able to correct in a second attempt. Meanwhile it seemed to him that these notes might be useful to him with the girl. The stuff might not go down with one like himself, who had had to listen to the preaching of morality times out of number ever since he had been capable of reasoning. But the girl was probably tired by now of many things of this world, though not of morality. Perhaps words which he had written from his heart, though when he read them over they awakened no emotion in him, might touch her.

That night also was restless, but not unpleasantly so. Prolonged sleeplessness always produces a little delirium. Not all the brain cells remain awake. Some realities disappear, and those that remain alive develop without check. The old man smiled at himself as a great writer. He knew he had something to say to the world, but in that state between sleep and wakefulness he was not quite sure what it was. Yet he was conscious that he was half asleep and also that day would come and the daylight to complete his mind.

When at last, towards morning, he fell asleep, he had a dream which began well and ended badly. He was in the midst of a crowd of men ranged in a circle on the large drill-ground. He introduced the girl to them all, dressed in her bright-coloured old clothes, and everyone applauded him, as if it was he who had made her so pretty. Then she seized a trapeze which, fastened to a trolley, went round in a circle right over all these people. And as she went by everyone stroked her legs. He also was anxiously waiting for the legs to caress them, but they never reached him and when they did reach him he did not want them any more. Then all the people began to shout. They shouted one word only, but he did not hear it till he was compelled to shout also. The word was, Help.

He awoke, bathed in a cold sweat: the angina in all its force crucified him on the bed. He was dying. In the room death was represented only by a beating of wings. It was death itself that had made its way into him together with the venomous sword, which was bending in his arm and his chest. He was all pain and fear. Later he thought that his despair had been increased by remorse at the disgusting dream. But in his great pain all the feelings which had darkened his soul throughout his life became intelligible and therefore also his adventure with the girl.

When the pain and the fear went, he began to consider once again the subject that occupied all his thoughts. Perhaps he hoped by this means to begin a great cure. How important was the part played by the girl in his life. It was on her account that he had been taken ill. Now she was persecuting him in his dreams and threatening him with death. She was more important than everyone else and than all the rest of his life. Even what he despised in her was important. The very legs which in their reality had filled him with indignation had corrupted him in his dream. In the dream she had appeared dressed in bright-coloured old clothes, but her legs had been those of the day before, clothed in silk stockings.

The doctor came with his usual prescriptions and his usual confident calm, imperturbable so long as he had to do with the angina, intent only upon the cure. He declared that this would be the last attack. The great pain was, in fact, a favourable symptom, seeing that debilitated organisms are not subject to great pain. Then: Fine weather would soon be here. The war was certainly coming to an end and the old man could go to some good spa.

His nurse did not forget to tell the doctor of the visitor the old man had entertained on the previous day. The doctor smiled and advised that there should be no more visits of the kind till he gave his permission.

With manly decision the old man refused to obey. The doctor must cure him without any prohibitions. The visits could not have done him any harm, and he resented the idea as an insult. In the future he should invite the girl to come and see him and he would see her often. The doctor might, had he wished, have discovered for himself that her visits could not do him harm.

The old man's behaviour on the very day after having suffered so much was a display of really noble heroism. He himself felt that he was giving proof of strength. The others could not know that the violent angina was not the most important adventure of that night. His life must not be carried on in the old convalescent style any longer. It must become more intense and less narrow, because his thoughts could not centre in his own poor self. He meant to follow strictly the doctor's prescriptions, but he believed that he knew something else which was important for the recovery of his health, and which he would not tell the doctor.

The doctor did not argue, because, good practical man that he was, he did not believe in the curative effects of argument.

Relief from a great pain is a great delight, and the old man lived upon it for that day. Freedom to move and to breathe is a real happiness for one who has been deprived of it, even if only for a few minutes. However, he found time to write that very day to the girl. He sent her the money he had intended to give her since the day before and informed her that he would send her more in the future. He begged her not to come to him until he sent for her, as he had been taken ill.

He knew now that he loved the girl of the bright-coloured old clothes and loved her as a daughter. She had been his in fact, as she had been in his dream, or rather in two dreams. In both dreams, remarked the old man to himself, not being aware that dreams occur at night and are completed by day, there had been great suffering, which was perhaps the cause of the illness with which he was seized, the suffering of compassion. Such had been the girl's fate, and he had played his part in it. It was his fault that she had walked the streets with the bell fastened to her feet to attract attention, or, actually tied to a trolley, had made the round of that circle, offering herself to the eyes and the hands of the men. It did not matter that the girl who had come to see him the previous day had failed to awaken in him any feeling of pity or affection. That was what she was like now, and he must save her, changing her, so as to make her become once again the dear, good girl who, alas! had been his, and whom he now loved for her weakness.

How much pleasure he got from his purpose, a pleasure that invaded every fibre! It affected everything and everybody, even his nurse, nay, even his old illness, which he thought he would be able to fight.

On the following day he sent for his lawyer and made a will. Except for a few legacies, which seemed important to him, but which were insignificant in comparison with his estate, he left everything he possessed to the girl. At least she would no longer be under the necessity of selling herself.

The girl's education was to commence when he had picked up in health sufficiently to be able to undertake it. He spent some days in revising the notes which he had made the previous day, and which were to be the foundation of the moral lectures he proposed giving her. Then he tore them up, not feeling satisfied with them. He had now completely diagnosed the fault committed by them both, which had been the cause of his illness and her ruin. It was not the fact that he had not paid enough for her love or that he had abandoned the girl which should give him cause for regret. His mistake had been in accosting her in the way he did. That was the error he must study. So he began to draw up fresh notes on the relations that were permissible and possible between the old and the young. He felt that he had no right to forbid the girl to love. Love might still be moral for her, but he must forbid her all irregular relations, and above all relations with old men. For some time he tried to include in his notes besides the old men an order to avoid also the young rake with the smart umbrella whom he had not yet got out of his mind. This complicated his task, and made his notes less sure and direct. Then the young man disappeared from his notes and there remained, face to face, only the old man and the young girl.

Time passed, and he never felt ready to send for the girl. He had written a great deal, but he must get some order into his notes, so that they might be ready to hand at the moment when he wanted them. Every week he sent the girl, through his own confidential clerk, a fixed sum, and wrote to her that he was not yet well enough to see her. The nice old man believed that he was speaking the truth, and it was true that he was not quite well, but he was certainly no worse than he had been before his last attack. Now, however, he was aiming at the complete health of an active man, and he had not yet reached that.

He felt better because he had recovered confidence. For a time this confidence increased regularly in a direct ratio with his attachment to life, that is to his work. One day, as he reread what he had written, there arose in the mind of the old man a theory, pure theory, from which both the girl and himself were eliminated. Indeed, the theory actually came into being through these two eliminations. The girl who was getting from him nothing but money soon lost all importance. The strongest impressions end by leaving in the mind only a slight echo which we do not notice or look for, and by now the old man was aware of the rising from the memory of the girl, whom he had loved and who no longer existed, of a chorus of youthful voices calling for help. As for himself, he underwent a double metamorphosis, as a result of the theory. First and foremost he became quite different from the selfish old man who had seduced a girl in order to enjoy her and not pay her, because he saw himself as one of a crowd of a thousand others who would gladly have done or did the same things. It was not possible to suffer for it. His own head stood beside thousands of other white heads, and beneath those hoary locks there was in each case the same evil look. Now he was transformed into something quite different from all the others. He stood on high, the pure theorist, cleansed of all evil by his sincerity. And it was an easy sincerity, because there was no question of confessing, only of studying and discovering.

He wrote no longer for the girl. He would have had to put himself on her own low level to be understood by her, and it was not worth while. He believed that he was writing for the world at large, perhaps even for the law-giver. Was not he examining an important part of the moral laws, which, in his view, ought to rule the world?

The confidence awakened in his mind by the work was boundless. The theory was a long business, and therefore he could not die till he had completed it. It seemed to him that he need not hurry. A higher power would watch over him in order that he might bring to a conclusion a work of such importance. He wrote the title in his fine, large hand: *Of the relations between age and youth*. Next, when he was beginning work upon the preface, it occurred to him that for publication he would have to have a beautiful vignette designed to illustrate the title. He did not see how he could put into it the footboard of the tram with the girl driving and an old man carrying her off from work. It would be hard, even for the cleverest of draughtsmen, to give clear expression to the idea by means of such elements. Then he had an inspiration—even an inspiration did not fail him. The drawing must show a boy of ten leading a drunken old man. He actually sent for a draughtsman to design the drawing at once. But he made a mess of it, and the old man rejected it, saying that, when he was quite well, he would himself look for an artist in the town to suit his purpose.

In the fine weather that had at last come, the old man settled down to work early in the morning. He gladly left his writing to go through the usual cures, because that did not mean an interruption of his work. Nothing could distract his thought which continued to progress and develop. Then he wrote again till lunch time. Then he had a short hour's nap in an arm-chair, a peaceful, dreamless sleep, and went back to his desk to stay there writing and thinking till the hour of his daily drive. He went to Sant'Andrea with his nurse, or, sometimes, with his doctor. He took a short stroll by the shore. He looked at the horizon, where the sun was setting, with a very different eye for the beauties of nature, or so it seemed to him, from what he had had in the past. He felt himself to be more intimately a part of it now that he mediated upon high problems instead of carrying on a business. And he looked at the coloured sea and the brightly polished sky, associating himself to a certain extent with so much purity, because he felt himself worthy of it.

Then he had supper and spent another hour enjoying his own work, reading over the pages that were being piled up in a drawer of his desk. In his bed, unsullied, with his theory as his companion, he slept a placid sleep. Once he dreamt of the dear girl, dressed in her brightly coloured old clothes, and in his dream he did not even remember the existence of the other girl with the silk stockings. With her he talked German, which she spoke intelligibly. Nothing exciting happened even then, and to him it seemed a striking proof of recovered health.

He would have liked to have someone at hand to whom he could read his work, checking it by the sound of his own living voice and by the expression on the face of someone else. But this blessing was not for him. He knew from the practice he had already had as an author that there was one great danger for his theory, that of getting out of the course set it by the facts. Many were the pages he tore up, because he had let himself be led astray in them by the sound of the words. To help him he had sketched out his point of view on a separate sheet, which he kept always in front of him: An old man is constituted in such a way that the power he possesses may prove harmful to the young man, who alone is of value for the future of humanity. This fact must be impressed upon him. But since he holds to the power he has acquired during his long life, he must use it for the advantage of the young. In his desire to stick to facts the moralist then referred in detail to his own adventure: It is essential to bring it about that the old man should not desire the pretty girl on the footboard of the tram, but should listen only to the appeal for help addressed to him by her. Otherwise life, now passionate and corrupt, would become pure, but cold as ice.

There followed a number of exclamation marks to bring out the difficulty of the task the moralist had set himself. How would it be possible for him to convince old men that it was their duty to look after like daughters, girls whom, if they were allowed, they would take as lovers? Experience taught that old men would show a heartfelt interest only in the fate of girls who had already been their mistresses. It was necessary to prove that it was not essential to pass through love in order to reach affection.

This was more or less the line taken by the old man's thought. Till now he had smiled at it, because he held that, as his methodical inquiry proceeded, he would be able to see the details of the problem more clearly.

He tried to draw his nurse into his work. All he wanted her to do was to listen to him. At his first words she flew into a passion: "So you are still thinking of that woman?"

Clearly any theory must die strangled if you begin by calling the girl who was its true mother that woman.

Then he tried the doctor. Apparently he liked the theory. The doctor noticed a real improvement in the old man's condition, and therefore could not fail to like a theory which he found useful. But it was hard for him to accept it in itself. He, too, old though he was, since he was in good health, looked at life with the keen desire of a person of intelligence and refused to admit that he was shut out from any of its manifestations.

"At bottom," he said to the old man, "you want to give us too much importance. We are by no means so very seductive." He looked at the old man and then he looked at himself in the glass.

"Yet we do seduce," said the old man, secure in his own experience.

"When that happens no great harm is done," remarked the doctor, smiling.

The old man also tried to smile, but the effort ended in a grimace. He, on the contrary, knew that a lot of harm was done.

Then the doctor remembered that he was first of all a doctor and stopped discussing the theory, that is to say the medicine which he himself considered to be important. He even wanted to help the theory, to play a part in it, but it was natural that his touch should destroy the old man's illusions. "If you like," he told the old man, "I will get you a book called *The Old Man*. Old age is treated in it as a disease, it is true, but one which does not last long."

The old man argued: "Old age a disease? A part of life a disease? Then what can youth be?"

"I believe that youth is not complete health either," said the doctor, "but that is another matter. Youth often catches diseases, but they are generally diseases without complications. In the case of an old man, however, even a cold is a complicated disease. This must have some significance."

"It proves merely that an old man is weak. In fact," cried the old man triumphantly, "he is only a youth grown feeble." He had found it. This discovery would have its place in his theory and would help it enormously. "Therefore, to prevent his weakness becoming a disease, the old man needs a thoroughly sound morality." Modesty prevented him from saying that his work would supply this morality, but that was what he thought.

This conversation with the doctor, which had proved so helpful to him, should have encouraged him to continue. But one day the doctor betrayed what he really thought so clearly that the old man realised that they had nothing in common.

One day, in the course of working out his ideas, the old man found himself obliged to go into the question of what rights old age had over youth. Great Heavens, the Bible had not been written for nothing. Did youth owe obedience to age? Respect? Affection?

The doctor began to laugh, and when he laughed he liked to reveal his inmost thoughts. "Obedience? Instant, because old men must not be kept waiting. Respect? All the young girls in Trieste on their knees to make it more easy to choose them. Affection? The good, solid kind, arms round the neck, or somewhere else, and lips pressed to lips."

In fact the poor old man had no luck. He had not found a kindred spirit. He did not realise that, as the doctor had not experienced the great attack of angina, he was not an old man like himself.

But even this discussion bore fruit, if only of a negative kind. Several pages already written were put in quarantine by the old man inside a white sheet of paper on which he wrote: "What does youth owe to age?"

Sometimes the theory got into a tangle and it was difficult to go on. Then the old man felt really ill. He had laid aside the work, thinking that a little rest would bring him the clearness he wanted, but the days ran emptily on. Suddenly death came nearer. Now the old man had time to feel the unsteady beating of his heart and to listen to his breathing, tired and noisy.

It was during one of these periods that he sent and asked the girl to come to see him. He hoped that seeing her again would be enough to reawaken his remorse, which was his chief incentive to write. But he failed to get the expected help, even from that quarter.

The girl had continued to develop. Smartly dressed, as on her last visit, she had evidently expected to be received with kisses. The old man was not very severe, not from embarrassment this time, but from indifference. By now he loved all youth of both sexes, including the dear girl in old clothes and even this doll, so proud of her dresses that she would talk about them in front of a looking-glass.

Indeed, she had developed to such an extent that she complained that the money was no longer enough and asked him to increase her allowance.

This called up the old man's business instinct. "What makes you think I owe you money?" he asked, smiling.

"Was it not you who seduced me?" asked the poor girl, doubtless carrying out the instructions she had been given.

The old man remained calm. The rebuke did not really affect him in the slightest. He argued the point, saying that it needed two to make love, and that for his part he had used neither force nor cunning.

She gave way at once and did not insist. Probably she was sorry and annoyed that she had spoken as she did, she who had always done her best not to appear mercenary.

To put her into a better frame of mind and in the hope of experiencing once again even a little of the old emotion, he told her that he had remembered her in his will.

"I know and thank you," she said. The old man did not point out the strangeness of the fact that she believed that she knew about his will, which had been kept secret, and accepted her thanks.

The talk was such a disillusion to him that he thought of making a fresh will and leaving the rest of his property to some charitable institution.

He did nothing simply, simply because theorisers are very slow when it comes to acting.

X   That is how the old man found himself alone, face to face with his theory.

Meanwhile the very long preface to his work was finished and was to his mind a magnificent success, so much so that he was always reading it over as a stimulus to further efforts.

In the preface he had only set out to prove that the world needed his work. Though he did not know it, this was the easiest part of his treatise. In fact every work that proposes to build up a theory consists of two parts. The first is devoted to demolishing previous theories, or, better still, to criticizing the existing state of affairs, whereas to the second falls the difficult task of building up things on a new foundation, and this is far from easy. It has been the fate of a theorist to publish in his lifetime two whole volumes to prove that things were thoroughly bad and unjust. The world was out of joint and refused to mend itself even when his heirs published the third posthumous volume, the object of which was to show it the way it should go. A theory is always complex and in developing it it is impossible to see it at once in all its bearings. Theorists appear preaching the destruction of a particular animal, cats, for instance. They write and write and do not at first notice that round their theory, as a necessary corollary, rats spring up wholesale. It is a long time before the theorist stumbles against this difficulty and asks in despair: "What am I going to do with these rats?"

My old man was still a long way from these troubles. There is nothing nicer or more fluent than the preface to a theory. The old man found that youth in this world lacked something which would make it even more attractive, a healthy old age to love it and help it. Plenty of work and thought had gone into the preface, because there he had to state the problem in all its aspects. So the old man began with the beginning, like the Bible. Old men—when they were still not so very old—had reproduced themselves in the young with great ease and some pleasure. As life was passed on from one organism to another, it was difficult to be sure whether it had been raised or improved. The centuries of history behind us were too short to give us the necessary experience. But after reproduction there might be spiritual progress if the relations between old and young were perfect, and if a healthy youth could lean for support upon a thoroughly healthy old age. Hence the aim of the book was to prove the need of health in old men for the good of the world. According to the old man the future of the world, that is, the power of the young who were to make this future, depended upon the aid and the instruction of the old.

There was also a second part to the preface. If he had been able, the old man would have divided it into many parts. The second tried to prove the advantage that would accrue to an old man from a pure relationship with the young. With his own children purity was easy, but his relations must not in any circumstances be impure with the companions of his children. The old man, if pure, would enjoy a longer and healthier life, which, in his view, would be of the utmost utility to society.

The first chapter was also a preface, for, of course, he must describe the actual state of things. Old men misused youth and youth despised old men. Young men passed laws to prevent old men remaining at the head of affairs, and on their side old men promoted laws to prevent the rise of young men when they were too young. Does not this rivalry imply a state of affairs harmful to human progress? What had age to do with appointments to office?

These prefaces, of which I give only the kernel, brought a good deal of trouble and a good deal of health to the poor old man for several months. Then there were other chapters which went easily enough and gave him no trouble, in spite of his weak state, the polemical chapters. One was devoted to showing that old age was not a disease. The old man thought he had been particularly happy in that chapter. How was it possible to believe that old age was a disease, when it was only the continuation of youth? Some other element must intervene to change health into disease, something which the old man failed to discover.

Then, according to the old man's plan, the work was to be divided into two parts. One was to treat of the manner in which society must be organised if it was to have healthy old men, the other dealt with the organisation of youth in such a way as to regulate its relations with old age.

Here, however, at every step the old man found himself interrupted in his work by the invasion of the rodents. I have already spoken of the sheets he had laid aside, wrapped in a piece of paper, meaning to begin work upon them again when some of his doubts had been cleared up. Many batches of other sheets had afterwards been sent to join them.

Thus he never forgot that money had played an important part in his adventure with the girl. For some days he wrote that money, which usually belongs to the old, ought to be confiscated to prevent its being used for purposes of corruption and it is astonishing how many hours elapsed before he realised how painful it would be for him to be deprived of his own money. Then he stopped writing on the subject and laid these pages aside in the expectation of receiving more light.

On another occasion he thought of insisting that even in the first class in the elementary school it should not be forgotten that the purpose of life is a healthy old age. When youth sins it does not suffer and it causes less suffering. Then the sin of an old man is equal to about two sins of a young man. It is a sin quite apart from the example he sets. Hence, according to our theorist, from the very first children should study how to grow old healthily. But then he felt that with such reasoning the path to virtue was not clearly blazed. If a young man's sin were so light a matter, where was the education of the old man to begin? And on the paper in which he buried these sheets he wrote: Must consider when the education of the old man is to commence.

There were pages in which the old man endeavoured to prove that, if old age was to be healthy, it must be surrounded with healthy young people. The system of setting aside sheets instead of destroying them helped the growth of contradictions which escaped the author's notice. These last pages revealed in the writer a certain amount of ill-feeling against youth. On the whole it was true that, if youth had been healthy, old age would not have been able to sin. Its greater physical strength already protected it from violence. On the sheet that enclosed so much philosophy was written: "With whom must morality begin?"

And the old man went on piling up his doubts with the idea that he was building something. But the effort was really too much for his strength, and with the return of winter the doctor also noticed a further physical decline in his patient. He made inquiries and ended by guessing that the theory which had done him so much good was now doing harm. "Why don't you change the subject?" he asked him. "You should put this work on one side and take up something else."

The old man would not take him into his confidence, and declared that he was just playing with the subject as a pastime. He feared the critic's eye, but he thought he would fear it only until he had finished the work.

This time the doctor's intervention did not have a good effect. The old man meant to settle seriously down to the work, solving one doubt after another, and began by returning to the question of what the old should expect from the young. For several days he wrote in growing excitement, then for several days he sat at his desk reading what he had written over and over again.

Once again he wrapped up the old and the new pages in the sheet on which was written the question he could not answer. Then he wrote wearily under it several times the word: Nothing.

* * *

He was found dead with the pen, over which had passed his last breath, in his mouth.

melville house classics

THE ART OF THE NOVELLA SERIES

THE CONTEMPORARY ART OF THE NOVELLA SERIES

THE CONTEMPORARY ART OF THE NOVELLA